I HAVE A FRIEND

by Michaela Muntean
Illustrated by Marsha Winborn

Featuring Jim Henson's
Sesame Street Muppets

A SESAME STREET/GOLDEN PRESS BOOK
Published by Western Publishing Company, Inc.
in conjunction with Children's Television Workshop.

I have lots of friends.
When we play hide-and-seek, I cover
my eyes and all my friends hide.

My friend Bird comes to visit me
when I have a cold in my snuffle.
He always makes me feel better.

My friend Grover does funny things.
He cheers me up when I feel sad. Yuh.

I have a friend who likes to count almost as much as I do. One friend and one friend make two. Ha! Ha! Ha!

My old buddy Bert likes me
even when I make him look silly.

I have a friend who will lend me
whatever I need, even if it's brand-new.

I have a friend who pops up
whenever I need him.

I, Grover, have a friend
who helps me try new things.
Oh, my goodness! It is not
easy to be a skating star!

My friend Ernie makes me feel brave
even when he's scared, too.

I have two friends who invite me to stay
for supper. I wish they didn't always
serve birdseed stew.

Friends are yucchy. I tell them
to go away and leave me alone.

But I don't mind when they bring me
a cake and wish me a rotten birthday.

My friend and I like to share
sodas at Mr. Hooper's store.

My friend Barkley always meets me
after school. He's very happy to see me.

My friend Ernie is a good sport.
He plays all my favorite games with me.
And he doesn't even mind when I win.

My friend Herry calls me every day.
We have a lot to talk about.

My friend Sully and I eat
lunch together every day.
I'm glad we're pals.

My friends and I have lots
of fun whenever we're together.
Do you have good friends, too?

ABCDEFGHIJKL